THE WIMP

Kathy Caple

1994

HOUGHTON MIFFLIN COMPANY BOSTON

To Christian

Library of Congress Cataloging-in-Publication Data

Caple, Kathy.
    The wimp / Kathy Caple.
        p.   cm.
    Summary: Arnold and his sister Rose give two bullying classmates a
taste of their own medicine when Arnold decides he doesn't have to
be a wimp anymore.
    ISBN 0-395-63115-7
    [1. Bullies—Fiction.   2. Brothers and sisters—Fiction.
3. Schools—Fiction.]   I. Title.
PZ7.C17368Wi   1994   94-7121
[E]—dc20   CIP
                             AC

Printed in the United States of America

WOZ   10   9   8   7   6   5   4   3   2   1

That day on his way home from school,
Arnold noticed Clyde and Watson following him.
"Nice hat," said Clyde.
He pulled Arnold's hat away.

"Give that back," said Arnold.

Clyde threw Arnold's hat over Mr. Green's fence.
"You'll have to go and get it," he said.

Arnold climbed over the fence and picked up the hat.

"Get off my property," shouted Mr. Green.

Arnold climbed back over the fence.

He landed in a puddle.

A few seconds later, Arnold's sister, Rose, walked by.
"You're a real mess," said Rose. "What happened to you?"
Arnold told her all about the hat and Mr. Green's yard.
"Clyde and Watson are out to get me," he said.
"I know it."

"Don't be such a wimp," said Rose.
"The next time they bother you yell 'GET LOST'.
Say it loud and like you really mean it.
They'll leave you alone. Believe me.
It's all a matter of knowing how to talk to them."

When Arnold got to school the next day Clyde and
Watson were waiting.

"We need to check your homework," said Clyde.
"GET LOST," shouted Arnold.
Clyde grabbed Arnold's bookbag.

He took out the homework.
"Give that back," said Arnold.

Clyde ripped the homework into tiny pieces and
threw it back to Arnold.
"Here you go," said Clyde.

Arnold went into class.

"Please pass in your homework," said the teacher.
"I can't," said Arnold. "It was blown away
by a band of robbers."
"Then you can just stay in for recess and do it over,"
said the teacher.

Arnold decided it would
be better if he stayed out
of Clyde and Watson's way.

During lunch period
he hid in the coatroom.

After school he hid in the library.
Arnold did not see Clyde and Watson sneak in.

They put a stink bomb next to his table and set it off.

"UGH! GROSS! What's that horrible smell?" said Arnold.
The librarian was really mad.

Arnold ran out of the room.

When Arnold got outside Rose was waiting for him.
"You look terrible," said Rose.
"What happened this time?"

Arnold told her about the homework. Then he told her
about the library and the stink bomb.

"I can't believe you actually hid from Clyde and Watson," said Rose. "What a wimpy thing to do. I'm going to show you how to handle those bullies myself.

Now, where are they?"

"Over there," said Arnold, "but I don't think you should bother them right now."

"Don't be such a baby," said Rose. "Watch this."

"Listen here you two," said Rose. "My brother says that you've been bothering him. You leave him alone or you'll have me to deal with. Is that clear?"

"Yes, sister," said Clyde and Watson.
They tossed some paint cans to Rose and ran away.

"See," said Rose. "What did I tell you. It's all a matter of knowing how to talk to them."

Just then the principal came out.
"You two are in big trouble," he said.

Rose looked at the paint cans. Then she looked at the wall.

"I tried to warn you," said Arnold.

The principal handed them scrub brushes and some smelly solution. "GET TO WORK," he said.

It took them several hours to get the paint off.

When they were finished they went to the janitor's room to clean up.

They heard a noise outside the door.
It was Clyde and Watson.

"We sure got Arnold," said Clyde.
"And his sister, too," said Watson. "Just wait until
they see what we plan to do next."

"You were right," said Rose. "They are out to get you.
And me too."

That afternoon Rose showed Arnold a different way to walk home.

The next morning Arnold and Rose left for school an hour
early. They took the long way.

But when they got to school

Clyde and Watson were already there.
"Watch this," said Arnold.

Arnold tiptoed over to the porch.

He picked up the ladder

and carried it away.

"See you later pals," shouted Arnold.

"Hey! We can't get down," called Watson.

"Help," yelled Clyde.

"Having trouble boys?" asked the principal.
He handed Clyde and Watson some scrub
brushes and smelly solution.
"GET TO WORK!"

"You really showed Clyde and Watson this time,"
said Rose.
Arnold smiled. "It's all just a matter of knowing
how to talk to them," he said.